The Secret Sea Horse

★ Also by ★
Debbie Dadey

MERMAID TALES

BOOK 1: *TROUBLE AT TRIDENT ACADEMY*

BOOK 2: *BATTLE OF THE BEST FRIENDS*

BOOK 3: *A WHALE OF A TALE*

BOOK 4: *DANGER IN THE DEEP BLUE SEA*

BOOK 5: *THE LOST PRINCESS*

Coming Soon

BOOK 7: *DREAM OF THE BLUE TURTLE*

Mermaid Tales

★Debbie★ Dadey

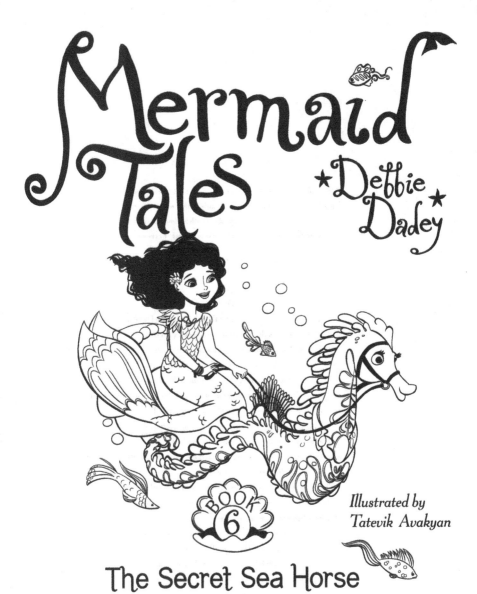

BOOK 6

Illustrated by
Tatevik Avakyan

The Secret Sea Horse

ALADDIN
NEW YORK   LONDON   TORONTO   SYDNEY   NEW DELHI

ALADDIN

An imprint of Simon & Schuster Children's Publishing Division
1230 Avenue of the Americas, New York, NY 10020
First Aladdin hardcover edition September 2013
Text copyright © 2013 by Debbie Dadey
Illustrations copyright © 2013 by Tatevik Avakyan
ALADDIN is a trademark of Simon & Schuster, Inc.,
and related logo is a registered trademark of Simon & Schuster, Inc.
For information about special discounts for bulk purchases,
please contact Simon & Schuster Special Sales at 1-866-506-1949
or business@simonandschuster.com.
The Simon & Schuster Speakers Bureau can bring authors to
your live event. For more information or to book an event contact the
Simon & Schuster Speakers Bureau at 1-866-248-3049 or visit
our website at www.simonspeakers.com.
Designed by Karin Paprocki
The text of this book was set in Belucian Book.
Manufactured in the United States of America 1020 SKY
4 6 8 10 9 7 5 3
Library of Congress Control Number 2013938155
ISBN 978-1-4424-8261-6 (hc)
ISBN 978-1-4424-8260-9 (pbk)
ISBN 978-1-4424-8262-3 (eBook)

To my Moland House friends:
Ed Price, Ken and Lorraine Barlow,
Clare Reilly, Mary Lutz,
Bob and Joy Snyder,
Murrie and Chaya Gayman,
Cal and Sandy Uzelmeier,
Warren Williams, Nancy Crowder,
Nancy Elias, Ginny Wolfe,
Toots Brown, Cheryl Lewicki,
Joan and Dave Healy, Ed Greenawald,
Dave and JoAnne Mullen, Chet Davis,
and Dawn Dickson

Contents

Contents

The Secret Sea Horse

The Worst Thing

ECHO REEF HELD HER BREATH. She crossed her fingers and her pink tail fins. She was hoping that Mrs. Karp wouldn't say the worst thing ever. But she did.

"Class," Mrs. Karp said, looking around the room of twenty third graders, "we will have a spelling test on Wednesday."

Echo's heart sank. But a merboy named Rocky Ridge cheered, "Yippee!" Everyone looked at Rocky in surprise. Usually he hated any kind of schoolwork.

Rocky smiled and then he laughed. "Just kidding."

Mrs. Karp raised her green eyebrows at Rocky, but continued. "Since we only have two days before your test, I'll give you a short list of ten words."

Ten words! Echo thought it might as well have been a million. Echo was a good merstudent in most of the subjects at Trident Academy. She liked merology, storytelling, science, and astronomy. But spelling was difficult for her.

Mrs. Karp pointed to a list of words on a seaweed chart. "These ocean creatures are extremely interesting. It will be quite useful to know how to spell their names." Echo looked at the list as Mrs. Karp called on various students to read the words aloud.

"Pipefish," Shelly Siren said.

"Sea dragon," Kiki Coral read.

Then Pearl Swamp read, "Sea horse." Echo *loved* sea horses. She couldn't help daydreaming about them. They were so cute and graceful. Sometimes she visited the Conservatory for the Preservation of Sea Horses and Swordfish, where her mother worked. Housed in the fabulous Trident Plaza Hotel, the conservatory had the largest display of sea horses known to merfolk. It was also a hospital for sick or hurt sea horses. Echo liked sea horses even more than she liked humans—and she adored everything about humans.

"Echo," Mrs. Karp said, "please read the next word."

Echo gulped. She'd been so busy thinking about sea horses, she wasn't sure which word were they on. She guessed and read, "Stonefish."

Mrs. Karp tapped her white tail on her marble desk and shook her head. "Echo, you need to pay closer attention. Pearl, please read the next word."

Pearl looked at Echo and stuck her nose up in the water before reading, "Trumpet fish."

Echo sighed. How was she ever going to learn ten new spelling words before Wednesday? She wished she could ride away on a sea horse and never take another spelling test ever again.

Gloomy

MERSTUDENTS FROM GRADES three to ten filled the cafeteria. Rocky and Adam sat at a table full of loud boys, seeing who could slurp the longest ribbon worm without breaking it. Echo, Shelly, and Kiki were in the lunch line when Shelly handed a folded piece of seaweed to Mr. Fangtooth, the lunchroom worker. "Mr. Fangtooth, we found this letter. I think it belongs to you," she said.

Echo recognized the note they'd found near the Manta Ray Express station a few days ago. "A nice lady dropped it by accident. We tried to give it back to her, but she swam away too quickly," she added.

Mr. Fangtooth opened the letter. His eyes got wide and he smiled, something he rarely ever did.

Without a word he dropped his big serving shell and swam out of the cafeteria. "That was weird. I wonder where he went," Kiki said as she helped herself to some ribbon worms.

"I can't believe it! I think we made him happy," Shelly said. "But someone else needs cheering up today."

Echo looked around the large lunchroom. Carvings of famous merpeople hung on the walls. Merstudents of all ages sat around polished granite tables with the gold Trident Academy logo in the centers. Everyone chatted in between bites of food. No one looked sad. "Who?" Echo asked.

"You!" Shelly said as the three mergirls sat down at their favorite table.

"Me?" Echo said.

Kiki nodded. Her long dark hair swirled in the water around her face. "You've been acting gloomy ever since Mrs. Karp told us about the spelling test."

Echo groaned. "You know how much I hate spelling!"

"Don't worry," Shelly said. "We'll help you."

Echo smiled. "Really?"

"Of course," Kiki said. "That's what friends are for."

Shelly took a bite of her hagfish jelly sandwich. She swallowed and said, "Okay, Echo. Let's get started. The first word is 'pipefish.' It's pretty easy. Just put 'pipe' and 'fish' together."

Echo tried it. "P-I-P-F-I-S-H."

"Close," Kiki told her. "You only left out one letter."

Echo groaned again. "It's so hard. I don't see why we have to have spelling tests, anyway. I've heard that humans don't have them."

"It doesn't matter, because you aren't human," Shelly said. "You are a mermaid, and you have a test on Wednesday, so you'd just better study."

Echo sighed. "What's the next word?"

Kiki thought for a minute. "I think it is 'sea horse.' Try 'sea' and then 'horse.'"

"That's the one I know how to spell!" Echo said. "S-E-A H-O-R-S-E!"

"Perfect," Kiki said. "I knew you could do it."

Echo smiled. "Wouldn't it be cool to own a sea horse?"

"Do you know the legend of the sea horse?" Kiki asked.

Echo and Shelly shook their heads.

Kiki grinned. "Then let me tell it to you."

The Sea Horse Legend

ECHO AND SHELLY PUT DOWN their sandwiches and leaned in close as Kiki started her story. "Sea horses once lived on dry land. They had four legs and a tail of hair that was just for decoration. They could hardly swim at all and carried humans on their backs over dry land."

"Humans?" Echo asked. "I never knew that sea horses carried humans."

"Me neither," Shelly said before wiping hagfish slime off her face.

Kiki nodded. "They were called horses then. Until one day, a big stallion—"

"What's a stallion?" Echo asked.

"A male horse," Kiki said. "So this boy horse walked along the shoreline in murky water with some of his friends, and quite by accident stepped on Neptune's tail."

Echo gasped. "You mean King Neptune? *The* King Neptune?" Neptune was the original king of the sea.

Kiki nodded. "Neptune was furious and swiftly touched the horse with his trident. The stallion reared up on its hind legs and tried to run away, but it was too late."

"What happened?" Shelly asked, her blue eyes wide.

"The horse's front legs disappeared and its rear legs turned into a tail. It got smaller and smaller until it was no longer than your hand. Then it plopped into the ocean and quickly swam away." Kiki finished her story and ate a handful of ribbon worms.

"But some sea horses are big," Echo said. "I've seen them at the Conservatory for the Preservation of Sea Horses and Swordfish."

Kiki nodded. "Yes, King Neptune changed the stallion's friends to sea horses as well, but some he kept large so they could pull his royal shell."

Echo closed her eyes for a second and imagined being in Neptune's royal shell carriage. She sighed and opened her eyes. "I don't care how sea horses came to be. I think they are amazing."

Rocky floated by their table with an empty lunch tray. "You're right, Echo. Sea horses are awesome. I know all about them," he bragged. "I have one at home."

Echo looked at him and laughed. "No wavy way." Rocky was always acting silly, and Echo figured this was just another one of his jokes.

"I really do," Rocky said. "I'm not kidding!"

"Then prove it," Shelly said, scrunching her nose. "We want to see it."

"All right," Rocky said. "Meet me in the front hallway when the last conch sounds after school. You can all come to my shell and I'll show you my sea horse. If you're nice, I might even let you ride him."

Echo gasped. Could Rocky be serious?

Zollie the Sea Horse

MY SEA HORSE IS NAMED Zollie," Rocky told Echo, Kiki, and Shelly, as the three mergirls swam with him to his shell later that afternoon.

"That's a funny name," Echo said, still not believing that Rocky actually had a real live sea horse. She was sure he was teasing them.

"Echo, it's not nice of you to say it's a funny name," Rocky said. "My grandfather was named Zollie."

Echo felt bad for making fun. Maybe Rocky wasn't joking. "I'm sorry," she said. You're right. It's a great name."

"Rocky, I should be home studying our spelling words," Shelly said. "If you're wasting my time, I'm going to be mad."

Rocky and his father, Mayor Ridge, lived at the farthest edge of Trident City in a big shell. When the merkids finally arrived, they floated to the back of the large home.

Rocky went around a smaller storage shell and pointed. "I'm telling the truth," he said. "There, that's Zollie."

Echo squealed. She couldn't believe her eyes. In front of them drifted a large, bright orange sea horse. It snorted and nuzzled Rocky's hand. Rocky gently rubbed Zollie's neck. The mergirls had never seen Rocky act so kindly toward anything!

"Look, Zollie's wagging his tail," Kiki said with a laugh.

Shelly nodded. "I'm sorry I didn't believe you, Rocky. Your sea horse is amazing." Zollie's head towered over them and his body was covered with big bumps. Echo

knew the bumps were quite normal for sea horses.

"How old is he?" Kiki asked.

"He's about five, which is pretty old for a sea horse," Rocky told them. "He was a birthday present. My uncle found him trapped in a human net."

"So he grew up wild?" Shelly asked.

Rocky nodded. "Yep. Zollie is one hundred percent wild sea horse."

"You are so lucky," Echo told him. "I wish someone would give me a present like this. All I ever get is glowing plankton for my hair." Echo did like shiny objects, but she'd trade all her sparkling treasures for just one sea horse.

"Would you like to ride him?" Rocky asked.

Echo looked at Rocky in disbelief. She'd always thought he was kind of cute, but now she thought he was the best merboy in the whole world. She was so excited, she could hardly speak. "Really?" she asked.

Rocky nodded. "Zollie is nice. I don't think he'd mind." In less than two mer-minutes, Rocky helped Echo get on Zollie's back.

"Are you sure this is such a good idea?" Kiki asked. "Maybe you should ask your parents first."

"Don't worry," Rocky said. "I ride him all the time. My dad said Zollie is the gentlest sea horse he's ever seen."

"Hold on tight," Shelly suggested.

Echo nodded and squeezed Zollie's leash tightly. "Now what do I do?" Echo asked.

"Just say 'giddyup' to go and 'whoa' when you want to stop," Rocky said.

Echo shrugged. "Okay. Giddyup!" she said.

Zollie raced off, with Echo screaming happily as she rode.

Echo Wants a Pet

"I T WAS SO MUCH FUN!" ECHO TOLD HER older sister, Crystal, that evening. "I never knew anything could be that exciting."

She was helping Crystal make crab popovers for dinner while they waited for their parents to come home from work.

"More than anything, I wish I could have a sea horse for a pet."

Crystal glanced up from her shell bowl of crab and shook her head. "That will never happen. Ever."

Echo looked at her sister in surprise. She knew their mother didn't like keeping pets, but maybe she'd make an exception. After all, Echo really, really wanted a sea horse. "What if I earned the jewels myself?" Echo asked. "How much do you think a pet sea horse costs?"

"There's no wavy way," Crystal said.

Echo put her right hand on her hip. "Why not?"

"Because sea horses are not pets. They shouldn't be kept on a leash!" Crystal snapped. "Sea horses should be free. How would you like to be locked up?"

"What?" Echo said, even though she had heard her sister. Crystal didn't say another word and neither did Echo.

At dinner, Echo didn't even mention Zollie to her parents. She could barely eat her crab popover. She kept hearing her sister's words: *Sea horses should be free.* Could her sister be right?

Later, Echo was supposed to be studying her spelling words, but she couldn't stop thinking about Crystal and Zollie. Echo tossed and turned all night. The next morning, she woke up extra early. She left a note for her parents and swam silently over to Rocky's before school. Zollie snorted when he saw her. Echo giggled when he nudged her hand. She patted his head. "Are you happy being a pet?" Echo asked him.

Unfortunately, Echo didn't speak the sea horse language. She was pretty sure Zollie didn't speak the mermaid language either because he didn't answer. But when she saw a big tear slide down his cheek, she got tears in her own eyes.

Prison

THAT'S QUITE LOVELY," MISS Haniver told Echo later that morning at school. "You show amazing artistic ability." The merkids were in art class drawing pictures to match their spelling words. Echo sure hoped it would help her remember them.

Echo was tired, but still grinned at her octopus ink drawing of a sea horse. She had never thought she was talented at art. Her sister, Crystal, was the one who'd won school contests with sculpting. In fact, Crystal's goal was to sculpt every sea creature in the ocean.

When Echo was finished with the sea horse, she went to the art station and got another piece of seaweed to draw a picture of the next word. A colorful poster about sea horses and razorfish caught her eye. She didn't care about razorfish, but read about the sea horses.

Zollie was a male sea horse. Echo couldn't help wondering if he had ever carried babies in his pouch. Then she had

CAMOUFLAGE
in the Sea

A razorfish has a long dark stripe along its body to help it hide among coral and sea urchins. Did you know razorfish swim with their noses pointed down?

The pygmy sea horse is often bright orange. The bumps all over its body help it to hide among sea fans. Did you know all male sea horses carry their babies in a pouch?

a terrible thought. What if he had children that were looking for him? Did sea horses keep in touch with their young like merpeople? Suddenly Echo felt horrible.

"Miss Haniver," Pearl complained, "Echo isn't doing her work and she's in my way. I need another piece of seaweed."

Miss Haniver peered through her tiny glasses at Echo. "I'm sorry," Echo said, swimming away from Pearl and back to her own artwork.

Echo picked up her sea quill, but she kept looking back at the sea horse poster. Before she knew it the class was over, and she had only finished drawing pictures for four words.

On the way to lunch Shelly whispered

to her, "You didn't study very much. You'd better finish this evening."

"I will," Echo answered. She was quiet until they were all at the lunch table. Suddenly she blurted out to Kiki and Shelly, "Can you speak sea horse?"

Shelly and Kiki spoke the languages of many different sea creatures, but they both shook their heads. "Why do you want to speak sea horse?" Kiki asked.

"I want to ask Zollie if he minds being a pet and kept on a leash by Rocky," Echo explained.

Shelly looked up from her lunch of spotted scorpion fish soup to answer, "Well, I don't know about Zollie, but I'd mind."

Kiki nodded. "I've heard that if a

merperson is captured by humans, they put them in a pen and never let them go."

Echo gasped. The thought of being trapped in some sort of prison would give her nightmares. What would it be like? What was it like for Zollie? She *had* to find out. She would visit him again right after school. Spelling would just have to wait.

End of the Ocean

GET YOUR FRESH RIBBON EEL!"
Echo called to the crowd
of customers at Reef's Fish
Store. She tried to be cheerful. Her family's shop was the last place she wanted to
be, but her father had insisted she help out
at the huge high-tide sale. They'd been

so busy that she hadn't had a chance to think about sea horses until Crystal put a lovely hatchetfish on the rock counter for a customer.

After the happy shopper left, Crystal asked Echo, "Did you think about what I said about sea horses?"

Echo had thought of nothing else, but for some reason she didn't want her sister to know. Echo shrugged. "A little."

Crystal wiped the rock counter while there were no customers and said, "Some creatures should not be pets."

"Why not?" Echo asked. All her life she'd dreamed of riding a sea horse. Why was that so bad?

Crystal frowned. "Because . . . because

they should be able to choose," she said.

Echo held up a ribbon eel. "This eel didn't choose to be someone's dinner."

"That's different," Crystal snapped.

"How?" Echo asked.

Crystal spun on her pink tail and swam over to the other side of the store without answering her little sister. A big crowd of people wanted the pickled spotted oarfish, and Crystal helped serve them. Echo knew she should help too, but she didn't. She just floated behind the eel counter and thought about Zollie.

"WHERE'S YOUR PLANKTON BOW?" SHELLY asked Echo the next morning on their way to school.

"What?" Echo asked, putting her hand where her bow usually went. "Oh, I forgot it."

Shelly looked at Echo strangely. Echo shrugged. She almost always wore glittering plankton to decorate her dark hair. In fact, she had tried many times to get Shelly to wear it too. But this morning Echo had totally forgotten.

"I can't stop thinking about Rocky's sea horse," Echo told her friend as they floated past MerPark. "I was even going to go visit him yesterday after Tail Flippers practice, but my dad made me help out at the store."

"I hope you had time to study your spelling words," Shelly said.

"Oh no!" Echo said, scooting to a stop. "I forgot all about the spelling test today."

"How could you forget?" Shelly asked.

Echo looked ready to cry. "Every time I started to study, I thought about Zollie."

"Sweet seaweed!" Shelly said.

"What am I going to do?" Echo wailed.

"Let's study on our way," Shelly suggested, pulling Echo toward school. "The first word is pipefish."

Echo concentrated. "P-I-P-F-I-S," she said.

Shelly frowned. "No. Sound out 'pipe' and 'fish.' Let's try another one. How about sea dragon?"

Echo took a deep breath and tried again. "C D-R-A-G-U-N! Is that right?"

"Close," Shelly said.

"What am I going to do?" Echo squealed. "I don't know any of them, except for sea horse. Oh, how I wish I had studied!"

"It's not the end of the ocean," Shelly said. "We'll study the rest of the way to school."

"I hope that's enough," Echo said, but she had a terrible feeling it wouldn't be enough at all.

8

Right or Wrong?

ECHO COULDN'T BELIEVE IT WHEN she saw her spelling test. At the top of the page was a big zero in octopus ink. She hadn't gotten one single word right!

Unfortunately, Pearl saw Echo's test too. "Echo missed every word!" Pearl shrieked.

"That's terrible!"

"Pearl, please keep your eyes on your own work!" Mrs. Karp said sharply. Echo put her arms over her test and looked at Rocky. He grinned and gave her a thumbs-up sign. Rocky wasn't known for being great at spelling either.

Echo had been wrong. It wasn't a bad day. It was the worst day in the history of the ocean! She had never failed a test before. What would her parents say?

Echo sighed and took a quick look at her spelling test. She had even left the *e* off the end of 'sea horse.' Why did 'sea horse' need an *e* at the end? Echo shook her head. She definitely couldn't understand spelling. It made no sense. But, of course, she hadn't really studied as

hard as she should have because she kept thinking of Zollie.

"Mrs. Karp," Echo said, "I have a question that's sort of about our spelling words." She paused. "Is it wrong to keep sea horses captive? My sister says it is."

"Hey, what's the big idea?" Rocky snapped. "I thought you liked Zollie. See if I ever let you ride him now!"

"I'm not asking to be mean," Echo explained. "I just want to know." She did want to know what Mrs. Karp thought, but now she felt really miserable. Rocky would never let her ride Zollie again!

Mrs. Karp tapped her chin with her white tail. "That is an excellent and important question," she said. "Let's see how the class feels. Raise your hand if you think it is okay to keep sea horses as pets."

About half the merclass raised their hands, including Rocky, Adam, and Pearl. Rocky stuck his tongue out at Echo.

"Now, who thinks it is wrong to keep sea horses on a leash?" Mrs. Karp asked.

The rest of the merclass lifted their hands, including Shelly and Kiki. Echo slowly held up her hand, although she wasn't exactly sure what she believed. She told Mrs. Karp, "I don't know what to think. I just want the answer. Is it wrong or not?"

Mrs. Karp looked at the third graders.

"I can't tell you what to think, Echo. Or you, Rocky. But the more all of you know, the better decisions you can make."

That may have been a good answer, but it wasn't the one Echo wanted.

9

Wild Creatures

WHY COULDN'T MRS. Karp just answer the question? Why didn't she just say keeping sea horses is okay ... or not?" Echo asked Shelly.

It was the next morning as the mer-girls swam to school. Echo had been mad at Mrs. Karp since yesterday. Echo had also been upset with herself for lots of reasons. She felt horrible that she'd made Rocky feel bad about having a pet sea horse. She'd also made him so angry that he would never let her ride Zollie again. And she'd managed to miss every word on her spelling test! She wished she could start this whole week over again. This time she would definitely study.

Shelly floated past a merstatue in MerPark. "Well, maybe it's one of those questions that's hard to answer," she said.

"Teachers are supposed to know everything," Echo snapped. Then she felt horrible for being mean to Shelly.

Shelly didn't seem to mind. She put her hand on Echo's shoulder and said, "Mrs. Karp said our guest speaker will help us."

At the end of school yesterday, Mrs. Karp had told the merclass she would invite a special guest to discuss sea horses with them. Hopefully the guest could come on short notice. Echo wanted some answers and she wanted them now. What she didn't want was the surprise she got.

"Mom!" Echo said when she saw her mother in her third-grade classroom. What was *she* doing here? Suddenly Echo was worried. Did Mrs. Karp call her mother in to speak to her about the zero on her spelling test? Echo knew she was in big trouble now!

"Good morning, Echo," Mrs. Karp said. "I've asked your mother to help us continue our discussion on sea horses."

Echo was relieved she wasn't in trouble. As the rest of the merclass swam into the room and sat at their desks, Echo read the poster at the front of their classroom: *SEA HORSES: Pets or Free?*

"Class, I'd like to introduce you to Dr. Eleanor Reef. She runs the Conservatory for the Preservation of Sea Horses and Swordfish. Some of you may have visited it. Dr. Reef is also Echo's mother." Mrs. Karp paused to nod at Echo.

Out of the corner of her eye, Echo saw Pearl and Rocky frown at her. Echo stared straight ahead and wondered what her mother was going to say.

"I'm delighted to visit your classroom. I thank Mrs. Karp for inviting me. She mentioned that you've had some questions about sea horses," Dr. Reef said. "The Conservatory for the Preservation of Sea Horses and Swordfish doesn't believe in keeping wild creatures as pets."

Finally, someone had answered Echo's question. Why didn't she think to ask her mom at dinner last night?

"But," her mother continued, "the problem is the definition of what exactly is a wild creature."

SEA HORSES:
Pets or Free?

"Rocky is a wild creature," Pearl said with a giggle. But she quieted down with a glance from Mrs. Karp.

"Wild creatures can be a danger to merpeople. They often carry diseases as well," Echo's mother said. "Some people would argue that sea horses aren't wild, but domesticated."

"What's that?" Rocky blurted.

"That's when animals have been kept as pets for thousands of years," Mrs. Karp explained.

Kiki raised her hand. "Dr. Reef, are sea horses endangered?"

Echo's mom nodded. "Yes, and some people feel that keeping them as pets may protect them from extinction. That is a good point."

"That's right," Rocky's friend Adam said in agreement.

"But," Echo's mom continued, "we must also consider if the animal depends on merpeople for food. Can it live on its own or does it need us to survive?"

Echo looked at Rocky. She knew he was thinking the same thing she was. Did Zollie need him? Or could Zollie live on his own and be happier free?

Second Chance

ECHO WANTED TO ASK HER DAD what he thought about sea horses, but he worked late. She already knew how her mom and Crystal felt. She went to her bedroom early and drew seaweed pictures of sea horses, large and small. She drew some with four legs. By the time she went to bed, her hands were covered with octopus ink.

She was tired, but she couldn't sleep. Her sea fan bed felt lumpy as she twisted back and forth. She couldn't get Zollie out of her mind. Did he hate being Rocky's pet or not?

THE NEXT MORNING, SHE FORGOT HER glowing plankton hair bow again. She even forgot her breakfast of parrotfish pancakes. She knew she had to see Zollie before school began. She needed to be careful because if Rocky saw her, he'd really get mad. After all, she was the one who'd started asking questions about whether keeping a sea horse was right.

Without making a bubble, Echo floated around Rocky's big shell and the smaller shell behind it. She couldn't believe what she saw. Rocky gently hugged Zollie before unleashing him. Zollie nudged Rocky one last time before galloping away.

Echo wanted to scream, "Stop," but she

didn't. Maybe it was better if Zollie was free. But if it was for the best, why did Echo feel so sad?

Rocky turned toward her with tears in his eyes. When he saw Echo, he screamed, "What are you doing here? I should have kept Zollie a secret. This is all your fault!"

Echo rushed off. She didn't stop until she sat in her chair at school. She put her head down to keep her friends from seeing the tears on her cheeks. What had she done?

At lunch, Shelly and Kiki tried to get her to eat. "Look, Mr. Fangtooth made white-sea-whip pudding," Kiki told Echo. "He must be in a great mood." Ever since they had returned his letter the other day, he seemed happy. That was unusual. Mr. Fangtooth was normally very grumpy.

"I'm not hungry," Echo told her friends. "Rocky will never forgive me. I made him give up his best friend!"

Shelly tried to cheer her up. "Don't be upset. Rocky won't be mad forever."

Echo's eyes brimmed with tears. "But what about Zollie? Do you think he'll be okay?"

Shelly looked at Kiki and the two friends smiled at Echo. "Sure. Rocky said Zollie was caught as an adult, so he lived on his own before," Kiki said. "I'm sure he's fine."

Echo felt a little better, but she still could only drink a bit of seaweed juice. She almost spit up the juice when she had a terrible thought. Didn't Rocky say Zollie was old? Maybe he was too old to be in the wild.

"Would you like to come to my dorm room after school?" Kiki asked. Shelly and Echo lived in Trident City, but Kiki's family was so far away she lived in the Trident Academy dormitory.

Echo shook her head. "Not today."

"Don't worry," Shelly told her. "You'll feel better tomorrow."

"I sure hope so," Echo told her friends. She felt terrible. And she realized Rocky probably felt worse. If she had a pet, she'd be mad if someone suggested she set him free. And she worried about Zollie. She hoped he was safe.

Echo still didn't know if it was right to keep a pet sea horse. She still didn't know how to spell "pipefish." But she knew there was something she had to do after school: She had to apologize to Rocky.

After swimming home, Echo watched

Shelly float off toward her apartment at the People Museum. As soon as Shelly was out of sight, Echo took off for Rocky's shell. What would he say to her? Would he yell? It made Echo want to turn around and hide, but she didn't.

The closer she got to Rocky's, the more worried she became. "This was not a good idea," she whispered to herself. "I should go home."

Still, she bravely knocked on the side of Rocky's shell. Nothing happened. No one came to the front sea curtain. Just as Echo was about to give up she heard a noise coming from behind the big shell.

She swam to the back and was amazed!

"I can't believe it!" Echo cheered. Zollie

had returned! Not only that, but he'd brought a friend. Zollie was in his pen, nuzzling a female sea horse.

Rocky swam up beside Echo. "Did you see?" he said with a huge grin.

Echo giggled. "Zollie came back!" He had chosen to be Rocky's pet!

"With a friend. What do you think we should name her? You want to ride?" Rocky blurted.

"Yes!" Echo squealed. "How about Pinky? She's such a pretty pink and yellow."

Echo sat on Pinky's back and Rocky

got on Zollie. Together they rode around Trident City.

Echo waved when they trotted by Pearl. Pearl floated with her hands on her hips and a huge frown on her face, but Echo didn't care. She was so happy. She had gotten a second chance to know a sea horse. It was almost like having one of her very own.

"Hey, Rocky," Echo said. "Do you think Mrs. Karp will give us another try on our spelling test?"

Rocky looked at her and shrugged. "Maybe."

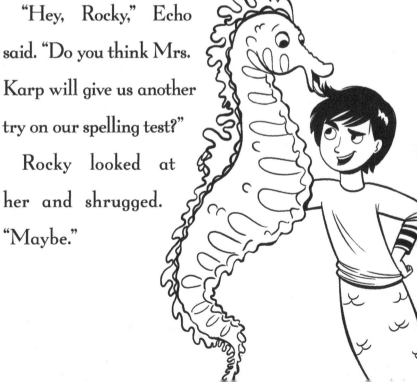

Echo made up her mind to ask her teacher tomorrow. Even if Mrs. Karp wouldn't let them take the test again, Echo vowed to study very hard for the next one.

Echo knew sometimes mermaids don't get a second chance, but, luckily for her, sometimes they do.

Class Drawings

✶ ★ ✶

Drawing of a pipefish by Shelly Siren

Drawing of a sea horse
by Echo Reef

Echo

Shelly

Rocky

Drawing of a
stonefish by Rocky Ridge

Drawing of a sea dragon by Kiki Coral

Drawing of a trumpet fish by Pearl Swamp

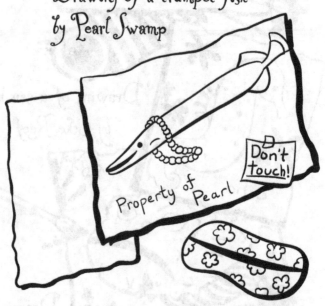

The Mermaid Song — Tales

REFRAIN:

Let the water roar

Deep down we're swimming along

Twirling, swirling, singing the mermaid song.

VERSE 1:

Shelly flips her tail

Racing, diving, chasing a whale

Twirling, swirling, singing the mermaid song.

VERSE 2:

Pearl likes to shine

Oh my Neptune, she looks so fine

Twirling, swirling, singing the mermaid song.

VERSE 3:

Shining Echo flips her tail

Backward and forward without fail

Twirling, swirling, singing the mermaid song.

VERSE 4:

Amazing Kiki

Far from home and floating so free

Twirling, swirling, singing the mermaid song.

Author's Note

A LEGEND IS A STORY THAT IS usually based on a true event in history. Often the story is handed down from generation to generation. I made up the legend of the sea horse in this story. I challenge you to make up your own legend. Maybe you'll make it about another sea creature, like how an octopus got so many arms, or perhaps you'll make up a legend telling how the ocean got so salty. I hope you'll share your legends with me. You can send them to me at Simon & Schuster, 1230 Avenue of the Americas, New York, NY 10020. I look forward to reading your legends!

Swim free,
Debbie Dadey

Glossary

GREEN HUMPHEAD PARROTFISH: This brightly colored fish's teeth form a parrotlike beak.

HAGFISH: The Japanese hagfish lives in shallow water and buries itself in the mud.

HORSESHOE CRAB: The American horseshoe crab is more like a spider than a crab. It is active at night and eats anything it can find, like small worms and algae.

LOVELY HATCHETFISH: Although its name is lovely hatchetfish, most people would say it is quite the opposite of lovely. It has large bulging eyes and is so thin it is difficult to see head-on.

OARFISH: The oarfish is probably where sea serpent legends come from! It can grow to be thirty-six feet long (six times as long as a man) and can weigh up to six hundred pounds. It has a bright red fin on its back, a blue head, and a silver body with black spots.

OCTOPUS: When the giant octopus is scared, it squirts a cloud of purple ink.

PIPEFISH: The pipefish looks a lot like a snake, but it is related to the sea horse.

PLANKTON: Plankton live in open water and float freely with currents. Most are small life forms, but jellyfish are also plankton.

RAZORFISH: These long fish swim with their tubular snouts pointing down.

RIBBON EEL: Ribbon eels change colors during their lifetimes.

RIBBON WORM: Ribbon worms are also called bootlace worms. Sometimes they live under rocks. They are one of the longest animals known.

SEA FAN: The purple sea fan is actually a coral and grows very slowly.

SEA HORSE: Sea horses choose a mate for life. The male sea horse has a pouch that carries the eggs until the babies hatch. Pygmy sea horses are only one inch long. Short-snouted sea horses are only six inches long. Sea horses big enough to pull a mermaid carriage have never been found in real life. Sea horses usually only live to be about five, but can live longer in captivity.

SEA PEN: This sea creature looks surprisingly like an old-fashioned quill pen.

SEA SPIDER: The giant sea spider is a bottom dweller, and its legs can be ten inches long.

SEA DRAGON: The sea dragon is a master of disguise. It looks like floating seaweed, but it is a fish.

SEAWEED: Neptune's necklace is a brown seaweed that grows near New Zealand. It looks like a string of beads.

SPOTTED SCORPION FISH: This poisonous fish has large pectoral fins that it opens when it is threatened.

STONEFISH: The stonefish's sting can kill a

human. Another master of camouflage, this fish looks just like a rock! It lives in the Indian Ocean and western Pacific Ocean.

SWORDFISH: The swordfish's upper jawbone looks like a sword.

TRUMPET FISH: If you see what you think is a thin piece of wood drifting in the ocean, it might just be a trumpet fish.

WHITE SEA WHIP: Sea whips grow as a single tall stem and often live in groups.

FIND OUT WHAT HAPPENS IN THE NEXT . . .

Mermaid Tales

★Debbie★ Dadey

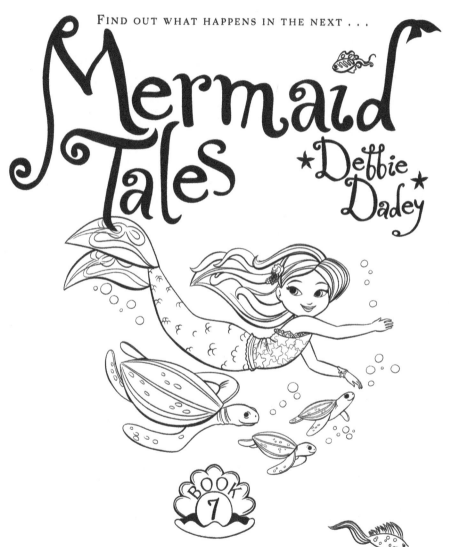

BOOK 7

Dream of the Blue Turtle

Leatherback Turtles

MRS. KARP, ARE YOU *sure* that's safe?" Pearl Swamp asked her third-grade teacher. Kiki Coral and the rest of the class waited for the reply.

"Of course," Mrs. Karp said, raising one green eyebrow as she responded to Pearl. "I wouldn't have asked a leatherback turtle to visit our school on Thursday if there was any danger."

"But aren't they awfully big?" Kiki asked. Her friends Shelly Siren and Echo Reef glanced at her. Kiki was one of the smallest mergirls at Trident Academy. She had been scared of whales because of their huge size.

Mrs. Karp nodded. "Yes, Kiki. Leatherbacks can weigh up to two thousand pounds and be seven feet long."

"And it's coming into *our* classroom?" Pearl said with her green eyes wide. "What if it sits on one of us?"

"We'd have smashed Pearl jam!" Rocky Ridge teased.

Several merstudents squealed until Mrs. Karp reassured them. "Marvin will not be in the classroom. We will meet him in the front hallway of the school, where there is plenty of room. Before we meet, I want you to prepare one or two questions to ask him."

"Marvin?" Rocky yelled. "What kind of turtle is named Marvin?"

"A very big one," Kiki said softly. Kiki knew leatherbacks weren't as big as whales, but something made her feel uncomfortable. She didn't know why.

"Marvin is a lovely name," Mrs. Karp told them. "Just as nice as Rockwell."

"Rockwell?" Pearl giggled. "Who is named Rockwell?"

"Nobody," Rocky said, but his cheeks were bright red.

Mrs. Karp continued. "Leatherbacks are the largest turtles in the ocean, class. They breathe air, so they can't stay underwater too long. They feed mostly on jellyfish."

"How do they get so big by eating just jellyfish, Mrs. Karp?" Shelly asked. "Jellyfish are made up of almost all water."

"It's a bit of a mystery," Mrs. Karp agreed.

"Maybe the mystery is that they eat mergirls, too," Rocky said with a laugh. This caused Pearl and several other mergirls to shriek in fear. Shelly just rolled her eyes at Rocky. He was always telling bad jokes.

"That will be enough out of you, Rocky

Ridge," Mrs. Karp said with a slap of her white tail on her marble desk.

Mrs. Karp went on to tell the merclass that leatherback turtles were endangered. "Floating plastic bags look very much like jellyfish. Sadly, the turtles don't realize their mistake until they've eaten the trash. If they eat too many bags, they can die."

The third graders listened to every word, but Kiki barely heard her teacher. Her eyes grew cloudy and her ears stopped up. She knew what was happening. She was going to have one of her visions.

Kiki covered her face with her hands. In her mind she saw a frightening sight: Rocky Ridge, an enormous leatherback, and swirling water! Suddenly she shouted,

"Mrs. Karp! I have to go see Madame Hippocampus! Now!"

The whole classroom stared at Kiki. "What is the meaning of this outburst?" Mrs. Karp asked.

Kiki twisted her hands together. She looked down at her purple tail. "I'm sorry. It's just that I need to see Madame right away." After what she had seen, Kiki desperately needed the advice of their merology teacher.

Mrs. Karp shook her head. "That is impossible. She is ill today."

Kiki gulped. What was she going to do? This couldn't wait. Not one more mer-minute.

Mr. Fangtooth

DO YOU SEE THAT?" SHELLY asked Kiki and Echo. "Mr. Fangtooth is smiling!"

The mergirls looked up from their lunch table to stare at the cafeteria worker. Mr. Fangtooth was usually very grouchy. Since the beginning of the school year, the three friends had tried to cheer him up. Once they had made funny faces. Another time they'd made silly noises. One day they'd told jokes. Nothing had worked. But today Mr. Fangtooth smiled and even whistled a cheerful tune as he cleaned tables and served food to the merkids.

Echo giggled. "I think he's happy. I bet he got back together with Lillian, his old sweetheart."

Shelly tossed a piece of seaweed called sailor's eyeball up in the water and caught it in her mouth. "I saw Mr. Fangtooth with Lillian yesterday at my Shell Wars game. They were holding hands!"

"It's so romantic!" Echo said with a giggle. She sipped her seaweed juice before saying, "Shelly, you were totally wavy yesterday. I cheered so hard when you made the winning goal."

"It was so exciting," Shelly said. "I thought for sure the Poseidon Prep School's octopus would block my shot. Did you see it, Kiki?"

But Kiki didn't answer. She was staring into a dark corner of the lunchroom. Her sea grapes sat untouched in front of her. "Kiki!" Echo said sharply. "What's wrong with you? Didn't you hear Shelly?"

Kiki jumped and asked, "What makes you think something is wrong?"

"Ever since Mrs. Karp told us about a leatherback turtle visiting us, you've been acting really funny," Shelly told her. "Are you afraid of leatherbacks because they're so big—just like with the whales?"

"At first I was," Kiki answered. "But I'm not afraid. I like leatherbacks. My dad even taught me to speak their language."

"Sweet seaweed," Shelly said. "Can you teach us a few words?"

"Maybe Later," Kiki said. She knew Shelly loved ocean languages, but right now Kiki couldn't think about teaching anyone anything. She grabbed her tray and sped away from the table.

"Where are you going?" Echo called after her.

"I . . . I'm not hungry," Kiki said, looking back at Echo. Kiki didn't know what do. She had never told her friends about her special dreams, or visions, of the future. Usually the dreams were good, but every once in a while they were scary. The one she'd had this morning had been horrible, especially for Rocky!

Kiki needed to speak to a merology expert like Madame Hippocampus desperately. Madame would know what Kiki's vision meant and what Kiki should do. But what if Madame was out of school the rest of the week? Would it be too late for Rocky?

As Kiki rushed away, she bumped into another lunch table. Her salad of sea grapes and sea lettuce splattered all over the Neptune, King of the Sea wall statue. A big blob of lettuce sat on his head like a slimy green hat.

"Oh my Neptune!" Pearl screeched from across the cafeteria. "Look what Kiki did!" It only took a second for Rocky to point and laugh. Pretty soon half of the merkids in the cafeteria were snickering at Kiki's accident.

"Echo, look," Shelly said, nodding at Mr. Fangtooth. He wasn't whistling anymore. And he wasn't smiling. He was swimming toward Kiki with a frown on his face.

"We have to help Kiki before Mr. Fangtooth gets to her!" Echo squealed.

"And then we have to find out what's really wrong with her."

Debbie Dadey

is the author and coauthor of more than one hundred and fifty children's books, including the series The Adventures of the Bailey School Kids. A former teacher and librarian, Debbie now lives in Bucks County, Pennsylvania, with her wonderful husband, three children, and three dogs. They live about two hours from the ocean and love to go there to look for mermaids. If you see any, let her know at www.debbiedadey.com.